GRAPHIC NOVELS

STONE ARCH BOOKS
a capstone imprint

Game day.

The Wildcats warm up for their season opener against the top-ranked Bandits . . .

Carlos Ramirez is the Wildcats' kicker.

THUMP!

Sports Illustrated KIDS

PRESENTS

KICKOFF BLITZ

A PRODUCTION OF

STONE ARCH BOOKS
a capstone imprint

written by *Blake A. Hoena*
illustrated by *Alfonso Ruiz*
colored by *Jorge Gonzalez*

designed and directed by *Bob Lentz*
edited by *Sean Tulien*
creative direction by *Heather Kindseth*
editorial direction by *Michael Dahl*

Sports Illustrated Kids *Kickoff Blitz* is published by Stone Arch Books,
1710 Roe Crest Drive, North Mankato, Minnesota 56003.
www.capstonepub.com

Copyright © 2010 by Stone Arch Books, a Capstone imprint.

Summary: Tou Yang is the smallest kid on his team, but he plays like a
Wildcat. Tou's job is to dash down the field and smash the ballcarrier o
kickoffs and punts, and he does it well. When the Bandits come to tow
an old enemy on the other side of the line goes out of his way to bring
down. Will Tou be able to overcome his gridiron bully, or will Darren se
him to the sidelines?

Cataloging-in-Publication data is available on the Library of Congress
website.

ISBN 978-1-4342-1909-1 (library binding)
ISBN 978-1-4342-2292-3 (paperback)
ISBN 978-1-4342-4948-7 (e-book)

Printed in the United States of America in Stevens Point, Wisconsin.
022013   007197R

WEEN THE STATE'S TWO HIGHEST-SCORING TEAMS, THE BANDITS AND THE WILDCA   SIK TICK

UP NEXT >>>

:02 SPORTS ZONE SPECIAL REPORT

:04 FEATURE PRESENTATION:

KICKOFF BLITZ

FOLLOWED BY:

:50 SPORTS ZONE
POSTGAME RECAP

:51 SPORTS ZONE
POSTGAME EXTRA

:52 SI KIDS INFO CENTER

SPECIAL TEAMS PLAY WILL LIKELY DETERMINE THE OUTCOME OF THE WILD... SIK TICKER

SPECIAL TEAMS ALL-STAR UP AGAINST FORMER TEAM!

Wildcats

TOU YANG

STATS:
TEAM: WILDCATS
NICKNAME: TINY TOU
AGE: 13
NUMBER: 25
POSITION: SPECIAL TEAMS

BIO: Tou Yang is almost always the smallest player on the field. But, as Coach Michaels says, "It's not the size of the dog in the fight that matters, but rather the size of the fight in the dog that counts." Tou may be tiny, but he leads the league in forced fumbles and total tackles. A former Bandit, Tou will line up against his former bully, Darren, when his Wildcats face off against the Bandits today.

CARLOS RAMIREZ

TEAM: WILDCATS
NUMBER: 7
POSITION: KICKER
BIO: Carlos Ramirez is a soccer standout who was recruited by Coach Michaels to play football. Carlos is the Wildcats' placekicker and punter — and he's also Tou's best friend.

BLZ vs BRS
3-1
TGR vs RDR
33-32
EAG vs BAN
14-7
SPA vs WLD
4-3
BAN vs RDR
21-15
RDR vs LIG
4-3
BLZ vs BRS
3-1
TGR vs RDR

DARREN BROODY

TEAM: BANDITS **NUMBER:** 46 **POSITION:** SAFETY
BIO: Darren is quite a bit bigger — and a whole lot meaner — than any other player in the state. He hits like a truck, and never lets up.

BROODY

TOM MICHAELS

TEAM: WILDCATS **POSITION:** COACH
BIO: Coach Michaels is calm, cool, and collected. Above all else, he is dedicated to the well-being of his Wildcats on and off the field.

MICHAELS

AARON TURNER

TEAM: BANDITS **NUMBER:** 12 **POSITION:** QB
BIO: Aaron is the state's top quarterback. He has an average of 250 yards passing per game, along with 17 touchdowns.

TURNER

Okay, Wildcats. You've shown what you can do in practice.

Now let's bring it to the game!

On three! One. Two. Three . . .

OOOOO WILDCATSSSSS

After the play is over...

Watch it, Yang.

THUNK

25

46

Darren?!

You can't hide from me, punk.

8

Looks like another special teams play.

That's fine. Darren isn't on special teams.

Now I can stop worrying and just have some fun!

But on the line of scrimmage...

Darren?!

Hey, runt.

At the start of the second half ...

SPORTS ZONE
POSTGAME RECAP

FBL
FOOTBALL

PNT
PAINTBALL

SKT
SKATEBOARDING

BSL
BASEBALL

BBL
BASKETBALL

HKY

YANG

WILDCATS

WILDCATS BEAT THE BANDITS WITH A LAST-SECOND TRICK PLAY!

BY THE NUMBERS

FINAL SCORE:
WILDCATS: 10
BANDITS: 7

GAME HIGHS:
TACKLES: YANG, 9
FIELD GOALS: RAMIREZ, 1
PENALTIES: BROODY, 4

STORY: Special-teams standout Tou Yang shocked every single fan when he scored the game-winning touchdown against the Bandits today. The risky play was a stroke of brilliance by Coach Michaels, since no one expected "Tiny" Tou to catch a pass thrown by the punter, Carlos Ramirez. The Bandits' safety, Darren Broody, was quoted as saying "Tou may be a little runt, but boy, does that kid hit hard."

UP NEXT: SI KIDS INFO CENTER

SZ POSTGAME *EXTRA*

WHERE *YOU* ANALYZE THE GAME!

Football fans went wild today when Tou Yang and the Wildcats outgunned the Bandits. Let's go into the stands and ask some fans for their perspectives on today's exciting game...

DISCUSSION QUESTION 1

Tou is the smallest player on the Wildcats, but that doesn't stop him from making big plays. How much does size matter in sports?

DISCUSSION QUESTION 2

Carlos Ramirez hopes to one day play professional soccer. If you could play any sport professionally, which sport would you choose? Why?

WRITING PROMPT 1

Tou has to handle the pressures of a bully *and* a big football game. When was the last time you felt pressure? How did you handle it? Write about it.

WRITING PROMPT 2

Carlos throws the winning touchdown in a big game. When was the last time you did something you were proud of? What happened? Write about it.

INFO CENTER

GLOSSARY

COVERAGE (KUHV-rij)—a defensive scheme designed to stop the pass, or a special-teams scheme designed to limit a kick return

LINE OF SCRIMMAGE (LINE UHV SKRIM-ij)—an invisible line that stretches across the field, separating both teams prior to the snap of the ball

MISERABLE (MIZ-ur-uh-buhl)—very sad, unhappy, uncomfortable, or dejected

OFFSIDE (awf-SIDE)—a penalty called when a player is on the wrong side of the line of scrimmage when the ball is snapped

RECOGNIZE (REK-uhg-nize)—to see someone and to know who the person is

RUNT (RUHNT)—the smallest or weakest member of a group. It is sometimes used as an insult directed at small people.

SPECIAL TEAMS (SPESH-uhl TEEMZ)—groups of players who are on the field during kicks and punts

VICIOUS (VISH-uhss)—cruel and mean, or fierce and dangerous

CREATORS

BLAKE A. HOENA › Author

Blake A. Hoena grew up in central Wisconsin. Later, he moved to Minnesota to pursue a Masters of Fine Arts degree in Creative Writing from Minnesota State University, Mankato. Since graduating, Blake has written more than thirty books and graphic novels for children. Blake currently lives in Minneapolis, Minnesota with his quirky dog, Zuki.

ALFONSO RUIZ › Illustrator

Alfonso Ruiz was born in 1975 in Macuspana, Tabasco in Mexico, where the temperature is just as hot as the sauce is. He became a comic book illustrator when he was 17 years old, and has worked on many Spanish graphic novels since then. Alfonso has also illustrated several English graphic novels, including retellings of *Dracula* and *Pinocchio*.

JORGE GONZALEZ › Colorist

Jorge Gonzalez was born in Monterrey, Mexico. Jorge began his career as a colorist for the graphic novel retellings of *The Time Machine* and *Journey to the Center of the Earth*. In 2006, Jorge helped establish Protobunker Studio, where he currently works as a colorist.

HOT SPORTS.
HOT
FORMAT!

GREAT CHARACTERS BATTLE FOR SPORTS GLORY IN TODAY'S HOTTEST FORMAT—GRAPHIC NOVELS!

ONLY FROM **STONE ARCH BOOKS** ▼

WAIT!

DON'T CLOSE THE BOOK!
THERE'S MORE!

FIND MORE:
GAMES
PUZZLES
CHARACTERS

www.capstonekids.com

STONE ARCH BOOKS
a capstone imprint